JEMIMA *Remembers*

BY CRESCENT DRAGONWAGON
ILLUSTRATED BY TROY HOWELL

Macmillan Publishing Company
New York

In the quest for mourning dove identification, via re-
membered bird calls, I would like to thank George
West, folklorist of talking traditions, of Little Rock,
Arkansas, and Georgann Schmalz, ornithologist, Fern-
bank Science Center, Atlanta, Georgia.

—C. D.

Macmillan Publishing Company
866 Third Avenue, New York, N.Y. 10022
Collier Macmillan Canada, Inc.

Printed in the United States of America

10 9 8 7 6 5 4 3 2 1

Library of Congress Cataloging in Publication Data

Dragonwagon, Crescent.
    Jemima remembers.

    Summary: Just before leaving for the winter, Jemima
visits one last time her favorite places on the farm,
recalling the wonderful summer she spent there with her
aunt.
    [1. Aunts—Fiction. 2. Farm life—Fiction.
3. Summer—Fiction] I. Howell, Troy, ill. II. Title.
PZ7.D7824Je 1984   [E]   84-855
ISBN 0-02-733070-2

For my aunt, Dorothy Arnof,
who has always given me
much to remember.

—C. D.

·FOR TRINA·

"Jemima?" says my aunt. "We're leaving soon."
"I know," I say. But I don't want to leave.

Everything says *leaving, going away:*
every door on the red farmhouse open wide,
every door on the white car open wide,
the suitcases in the hall,
the suitcases on the grass by the driveway.
My aunt looks at me and understands. "Well," she says,
"I guess you have time for one more walk."
"I'll be back in time," I say.
She says, "I know." The wind blows around us.
Then I go.

Down the hill, I pass the garden
where my aunt and I planted zucchini seeds from a packet,
three seeds to a hill of dirt, last spring.
I remember we planted tomato seedlings, too, from Allen's Farm
and patted the earth around each baby plant,
and watered them till the earth turned to mud.
They grew so fast!
And I remember the day I found the first tomato, green
and small, hard as a marble, and soon I found
big red tomatoes hanging hidden under the spicy-scented leaves
and fat green zucchini
lying like crocodiles in the shade
of thick, hairy green vines.
But now,
the zucchini plants are brown and limp
and the tomato plants have fallen,
and summer is over,
and we have to go.

I walk down the road toward the pond
and something in me is singing sadly
the last time, last time, last time,
and one single bird is singing
pweee-ooo-ooo-ooo, pweee-ooo-ooo.
Swirls of gray road dust
mix with the falling yellow leaves in the wind,
and I'm cold, even in my down coat.

How could the summer have been
as hot as I remember?
I remember walking down this same road
the day I had a sunburn. I was wearing a bathing suit, and thongs.
My shoulders hurt
and the maple trees seemed to droop in the heat,
their green leaves gray with dust,
and heat glinted from the ground.

I remember I stepped out of my thongs on the green wooden dock,
and walked to the edge of the pond. I leaned over, and put one toe in.
Then I climbed down the slanted wooden ladder and, rung by rung,
I felt the cool, cool water cover me.
How good it felt!

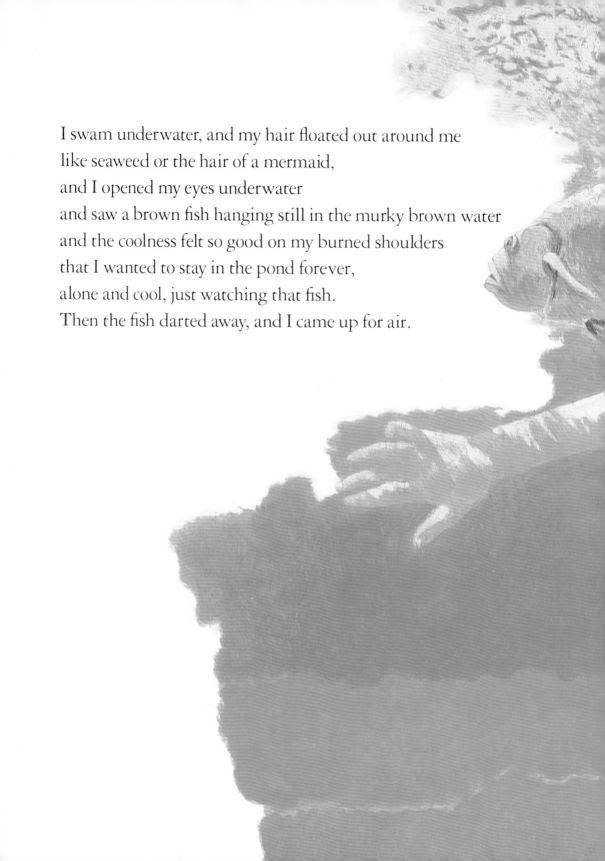

I swam underwater, and my hair floated out around me
like seaweed or the hair of a mermaid,
and I opened my eyes underwater
and saw a brown fish hanging still in the murky brown water
and the coolness felt so good on my burned shoulders
that I wanted to stay in the pond forever,
alone and cool, just watching that fish.
Then the fish darted away, and I came up for air.

But now the air is cold and wet,
pricked with tiny drops of rain, not hot and dusty.
And now the round pond
is dark, like a still, black mirror,
and the maple trees reflected in it
are yellow, red, and gold, not dusty green.
The water looks so cold now, I shiver.
Was it really here, on this dock,
that my aunt and I drank cider?

Yes. I remember.
I remember how the cider was half-frozen,
brown, and sweet, with little icy flecks still solid,
and how deliciously
it slid down my dry throat.
I sipped it, and I watched
my aunt dive into the cool water.
She never stuck her toe in first, just dove.
All summer long, she did that.
All summer long, I tested it first.

A crow goes *ca-aw, ca-aw, ca-aw,*
and I look up. It's circling in the cold sky
black as a splash of spilled paint
against the gray-white clouds.
I remember that sky blazing blue and summer hot.

When my aunt and I first came here,
the road was still muddy from spring rain
and black mud splashed
the white car. But the lawn was green
and I remember watching
a fat robin hopping on it.
I remember my aunt trying to open the door,
muttering, "This … stupid … *key!*" until
it turned and we went in,
and the sleigh bells on the door
jingled back against the wood,
one sound of summer,
summer back at the farm, my aunt and me again.
I remember how the house looked different from last year,
smaller or bigger than before, but I couldn't figure out how
since it also looked the same.
My aunt and I just stood there then, still
breathing in the old-wood smell.
Then we brought in the suitcases.

And now the hall is filled with suitcases again,
and we have to go.
I'm standing here by the pond
and I have to leave
and I don't want to.
I'm thinking *last time, the last time.*
I'm thinking *goodbye*, and *I don't want to go.*

I pull the belt of my coat tighter
and I remember what my aunt said to me
last night:

> *It will be waiting for us here, the farm.*
> *All through the winter,*
> *when the white, silent snow*
> *falls and falls again,*
> *when so much snow falls*
> *that it covers all the windows*
> *and presses in against the house,*
> *when the pond freezes solid*
> *and then that ice is covered with snow,*
> *and everywhere is only the silent, lonely white*
> *shadowed in gray and blue,*
> *the farm will still be here, waiting for us.*

I think, *We will come again.*

"Jemima? Time to go!"
I hurry up the hill to the packed car,
to my busy, pretty aunt in a red sweater.
"Cold!" she says.
"Yes," I say.
"I heated up the last of the cider with some cinnamon," she says,
"and put it in a thermos to drink on the way home."
"Good," I say. "And can we stop at Allen's Farm
and buy some of those doughnuts to go with it?"
"You bet," she says, and she smiles at me.
"I've locked the house up,
but if you want to go back in one more time…."

I shake my head.

"So you're ready to go now?" she asks me.

"Yes," I say.